Dear Parent:

Congratulations! Your child is taking the first steps on an exciting journey. The destination? Independent reading!

STEP INTO READING® will help your child get there. The program offers five steps to reading success. Each step includes fun stories and colorful art. There are also Step into Reading Sticker Books, Step into Reading Math Readers, Step into Reading Write-In Readers, Step into Reading Phonics Readers, and Step into Reading Phonics First Steps! Boxed Sets—a complete literacy program with something for every child.

Learning to Read, Step by Step!

Ready to Read **Preschool–Kindergarten**
• big type and easy words • rhyme and rhythm • picture clues
For children who know the alphabet and are eager to begin reading.

Reading with Help **Preschool–Grade 1**
• basic vocabulary • short sentences • simple stories
For children who recognize familiar words and sound out new words with help.

Reading on Your Own **Grades 1–3**
• engaging characters • easy-to-follow plots • popular topics
For children who are ready to read on their own.

Reading Paragraphs **Grades 2–3**
• challenging vocabulary • short paragraphs • exciting stories
For newly independent readers who read simple sentences with confidence.

Ready for Chapters **Grades 2–4**
• chapters • longer paragraphs • full-color art
For children who want to take the plunge into chapter books but still like colorful pictures.

STEP INTO READING® is designed to give every child a successful reading experience. The grade levels are only guides. Children can progress through the steps at their own speed, developing confidence in their reading, no matter what their grade.

Remember, a lifetime love of reading starts with a single step!

Special thanks to Rob Hudnut, Nancy Bennett, Tiffany J. Shuttleworth, Rick Rivezzo, Zoë Chance, Vicki Jaeger, Monica L. Okazaki, Phil Mendoza, and Mainframe Entertainment

www.stepintoreading.com
www.barbie.com

Educators and librarians, for a variety of teaching tools, visit us at
www.randomhouse.com/teachers

Library of Congress Cataloging-in-Publication Data
Landolf, Diane Wright.
Fairytopia / adapted by Diane Wright Landolf ; based on the screenplay by Elise Allen and Diane Duane. — 1st ed.
    p.   cm. — (Step into reading. Step 2) "Barbie."
ISBN 0-375-83696-9 (trade) — ISBN 0-375-93696-3 (lib. bdg.)
I. Allen, Elise. II. Duane, Diane. III. Title. IV. Step into reading. Step 2 book.
PZ7.L2317345Fai 2006   2005016629

Printed in the United States of America

10 9 8 7 6 5 4 3 2 1

First Edition

Barbie™ Fairytopia™

Adapted by Diane Wright Landolf
Based on the original screenplay
by Elise Allen, Diane Duane

Random House 🏠 New York

There once was
a magical land
called Fairytopia.

A sweet fairy
named Elina
lived there.
She had no wings.

Elina lived
inside a flower.

The pixies teased Elina.
They said
a fairy with no wings
was no use.

Her friend Dandelion
loved Elina anyway.

So did
her puffball, Bibble.

The Enchantress
ruled Fairytopia.
She was
a good fairy.

The Guardians
helped her.
They kept
Fairytopia safe.

But the Enchantress
had an evil twin.
Her name was Laverna.
She wanted
to take over.

The ugly Fungus
were her helpers.

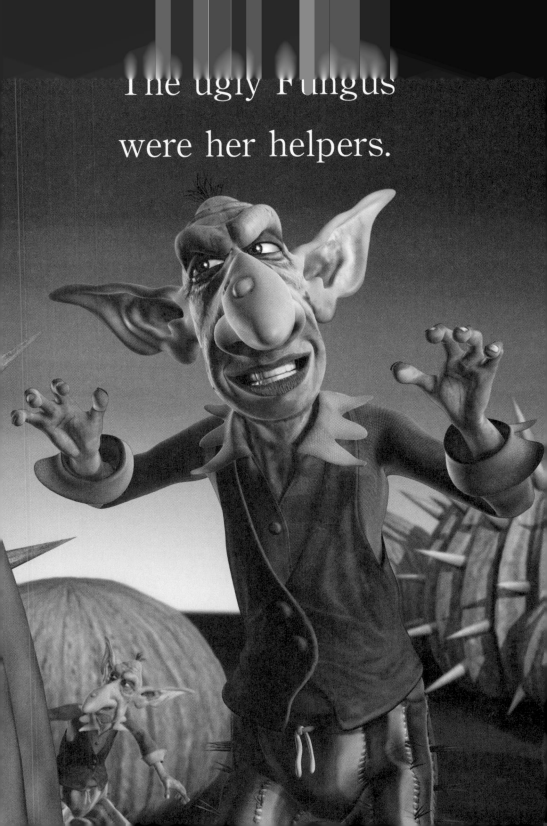

Laverna's brew

made the flowers sick.

It made

the fairies weak.

They could not fly!

But Elina was strong.

She could walk far.

She could get help

from the Guardian Azura.

Elina found Azura.
They had tea.

Azura told Elina
to find Dahlia.
Azura gave Elina
her magic necklace.

A butterfly
came for Elina.
They flew away
to find Dahlia.

But Laverna's Firebirds chased them.

The Merprince Nalu
helped them.

At last,
Elina met Dahlia.
Dahlia knew
Laverna's secret.

She said a crystal
held Laverna's power.
Elina needed
to break the crystal!

Elina found

Laverna's hideout.

She hid
from the Fungus.
Then she ran inside.

Laverna wanted
Azura's necklace.
She promised
to give Elina wings!

At first,

Elina was tempted.

Not for long.
Elina threw
Azura's necklace
at the crystal.

The crystal broke!

Laverna was gone.

Fairytopia was saved!
The fairies
could fly again.

The Enchantress
thanked Elina.
She gave her a gift.
It was a necklace.

All at once,
Elina had wings!
That was the gift
she wanted most of all.

If you can recognize familiar words and sound out new words with help, look for these Step into Reading books:

ALL STUCK UP
BARBIE: A DAY AT THE FAIR ✿
BARBIE: LOST AND FOUND ✿
BARBIE: ON THE ROAD ✿ ✎
BARBIE: TWO PRINCESSES ✿
BEARS ARE CURIOUS
BEAR'S BIG IDEAS ✎
BEEF STEW
THE BERENSTAIN BEARS
   BY THE SEA
THE BERENSTAIN BEARS
   CATCH THE BUS
BONES
BUZZ'S BACKPACK ADVENTURE ✪
CAT AT BAT
CAT ON THE MAT
COUNTING SHEEP ✧
DAVID AND THE GIANT
DINOSAUR BABIES
A DOLLAR FOR PENNY ✧
A DREAM FOR A PRINCESS ✪
THE EARLY BIRD
FIVE SILLY FISHERMEN ✧
HAPPY BIRTHDAY, THOMAS! ➤
HERE COMES SILENT E! ◆
HOME, STINKY HOME ✪
HONEYBEES
I LOVE YOU, MAMA ✪
IS IT HANUKKAH YET?
JAMES GOES BUZZ, BUZZ ➤
LITTLE CRITTER SLEEPS OVER
MICE ARE NICE
MOUSE MAKES MAGIC ◆
MY LOOSE TOOTH
MY NEW BOY

NO MAIL FOR MITCHELL
OH MY, PUMPKIN PIE!
ONE HUNDRED SHOES ✧
PEANUT
A PET FOR A PRINCESS ✪
PIE RATS AHOY!
PINOCCHIO'S NOSE GROWS ✪
PIZZA PAT
P. J. FUNNYBUNNY CAMPS OUT
P. J. FUNNYBUNNY'S BAG OF TRICKS
PLATYPUS!
A PONY FOR A PRINCESS ✪
POOH'S EASTER EGG HUNT ✪
POOH'S HALLOWEEN PUMPKIN ✪
POOH'S HONEY TREE ✪
POOH'S VALENTINE ✪
QUICK, QUACK, QUICK!
RAILROAD TOAD
READY? SET. RAYMOND!
RICHARD SCARRY'S
   THE WORST HELPER EVER
SEALED WITH A KISS ✪
SILLY SARA ◆
SIR SMALL AND THE DRAGONFLY
SIR SMALL AND THE SEA MONSTER
THE STATUE OF LIBERTY
SURPRISE FOR A PRINCESS ✪
THE TEENY TINY WOMAN
THOMAS AND THE SCHOOL TRIP ➤
TIGER IS A SCAREDY CAT
TOAD ON THE ROAD
TWO FINE LADIES: TEA FOR THREE
WHISKERS
WHOSE FEET?

✿   A Barbie Reader
✪   A Disney Reader
✧   A Math Reader
◆   A Phonics Reader
➤   A Thomas the Tank Engine Reader
✎   A Write-In Reader

STEP INTO READING

reading with help

It's time for YOU!
Pick your favorite
spot to read.
This is going to be
a great book!

What this book is about . . .
Barbie **Fairytopia**™
The fairy Elina has no wings.
The other fairies are sick and cannot fly.
Only Elina can save them!

Learning to Read, Step by Step!

Ready to Read Preschool–Kindergarten

Reading with Help Preschool–Grade 1
Does your child recognize familiar words on sight and
sound out new words with help? Step 2 is just right.
Basic Vocabulary • Short Sentences • Simple Stories

Readi̶̶̶̶̶ades 1–3

PQX626743

Reading Paragraphs Grades 2–3

To learn about
all the Steps,
turn to page 1.

̶for Chapters Grades 2–4

RANDOM HOUSE
www.stepintoreading.com
www.randomhouse.com/kids